4 2/11

THE LIFE AND MEMOIRS OF DOCTOR PI
AND OTHER STORIES

by Edgar Bayley
translated by Emily Toder

First published 2011 by

Clockroot Books
An imprint of Interlink Publishing Group, Inc.
46 Crosby Street
Northampton, Massachusetts 01060
www.clockrootbooks.com
www.interlinkbooks.com

Library of Congress Cataloging-in-Publication Data
Bayley, E. (Edgar), 1919–1990
[Vida y memoria del Doctor Pi y otras historias. English]
The life and memoirs of Dr. Pi and other stories / by Edgar Bayley ; translated by
Emily Toder.—1st American ed.
    p. cm.
Originally published as: Vida y memoria del Doctor Pi y otras historias. Buenos
Aires : Ediciones Ultimo Reino, 1983.
ISBN 978-1-56656-837-1 (pbk.)
I. Title.

PQ7797.B4125V4513 2010
861'.62—dc22

Original cover art by Daniella Brahms

Grateful acknowledgment to the *Massachusetts Review* and *Route 9*, where some of
these stories have appeared.

Printed and bound in the United States of America

The Life and Memoirs of Doctor Pi

Other Stories

Epilogue

THE LIFE AND MEMOIRS OF DOCTOR PI

The Charmer

I say nothing, I think nothing, Dr. Pi repeated to himself, without moving his lips, as he crossed the street. A blue deer and a helicopter briefly drew his attention.

He took out his umbrella and said finally in a very low voice:

"It was necessary."

A woman, plump and middle-aged, warned him:

"Careful, your shoelaces have come undone."

Pi thanked her for the warning and tied his shoes. Then he walked confidently toward the snake charmer.

She held out her arms to him and abandoned her stand at the fairgrounds.

"Only for a few moments," said the charmer.

"There is nothing but moments, a few small moments," said Pi.

The Bundle

"Careful. Careful with that package," said Dr. Pi.

The four men could barely manage and moved clumsily down the winding staircase.

"Don't stop moving, please."

It was clear that the bundle was getting larger and heavier. The straps around it grew tighter and the burlap of the case began to swell almost to the point of bursting. From inside emerged a grayish-brown gelatinous substance.

"Faster. We must hurry. If not, the espeletia resin will be the end of us," warned Pi.

One of the men stumbled and the suitcase fell on top of him. In this way they arrived at the first floor. A door opened and there stood a very pale woman with blackish hair wearing a sheer robe. She asked Dr. Pi to come in. He seemed to reflect for a few moments.

"Yes, that will be most appropriate. I will sleep with this woman. You bring the package down and give it to Enrique Molina, who needs it urgently."

The woman was called Etelvina. Pi removed his suit jacket and tossed his hat on the floor. Etelvina opened her robe and received Dr. Pi. Afterward, she told him that she had a young but melancholic lover who embittered her with his cheerless mood.

"This balm will cure him," said Dr. Pi, handing her a small green flask. He said goodbye to Etelvina and upon leaving ran into the sociologist M. Chombart de Lauwe.

"I see we're going the same way."

"I'm glad of it, Professor."

"I've always held," said the Professor, "that man makes choices in light of the facts of his situation. I've arrived at this conclusion on the basis of empirical research on daily life."

"Excuse me, Professor, but daily life does not exist," answered Pi. "I've arrived at that conclusion by virtue of my own empirical research."

"Can it be? So they had me fooled?"

"Have no doubt of it, Professor."

"I'm quite interested in what you're saying. Are you in a hurry? Would you like to join me for a cup of coffee?"

"At this time I cannot. I must oversee the transfer of a certain bundle, but if you'd like to come along, we can keep talking on the way."

Minutes later, they began their ascent from the ground floor. They left a guard at the camp and split up into two groups. The sleeping bags, parabolic antenna, the guitar, and all incoming correspondence stayed at the camp. The bundle and the sociologist were transported to the mountaintop by cable car.

The Message

Dr. Pi entered the motel. He would rest. Everything had been readied. Soon he would be in another land. First he had to receive a message. An answer to one he had sent. He looked around his room and noticed a green curtain. He drew it open. It was the entrance to a lit tunnel.

"That's good," said Dr. Pi. "It's been decided. I'll take a few pictures while the message comes in."

There was an underground rumbling.

"No, there's no doubt. This is the place."

An envelope slid under the door. Pi opened it. It was the message he had been waiting for. Someone had written *YES* in red. Pi undressed, took a bath, put on a diving suit and slippers and took off into the tunnel. He walked a few meters down a steep and very wide street, lined on both sides by storefronts, offices, and art galleries. A fat man, short in stature and wearing a large white lab coat, asked him into his office.

"I've got your solution in here."

"I'm not looking for solutions," said Dr. Pi, "I'm looking for a brunette."

"You'll never learn," replied the fat man, perturbed.

"Learning is not my trade," answered Dr. Pi, quickening his step.

The street's incline began to grow more pronounced. The slippers and diving suit became encumbering. He left it all with the fat man and proceeded onward nude and in great strides toward the end of the tunnel. There, beside the port, Beatriz awaited him in a canoe. Pi kissed her

intensely and quickly, and, grasping for the oars, said:
"We've got to get to the gulf before Edgar."

Of Poetry

The poet Madariaga had acquired a horse ranch. One with rare horses. Tall horses, short ones, tiny little horses yielded by subtle crossbreeding and highly refined techniques. His intention was not to train race horses, though he had some very fast ones, much desired by various studs. His apparent purpose was to yield new species of horses. Horses that wouldn't seem like horses at all.

He had stallions of several breeds: enormous, silent, impressive in appearance, and mares that were ardent, elusive, and curious all at the same time. He had day laborers and expert techniques and he also had a very ambitious project that he guarded in total secrecy. Yes, there was much activity at this ranch ("Don Eusebio," it was called).

At the end of the working day, over dinner, arguments—sometimes pigheaded ones—arose between the biologists and the zoologists and Madariaga.

"You're all lacking in imagination," Madariaga would say, "literary background, knowledge of mythology."

"Could be," they'd respond, "but we know what can't be done."

"Not only that; you believe to be impossible what was once possible," Madariaga would insist.

"There are limits to crossbreeding and hybridization, and, in any case, proper conditions do not exist for the emergence of a new animal on earth. Besides, we know nothing about the kind of animal you are aiming to achieve," they'd answer.

At this point in the conversation, Madariaga would fall prudently silent.

Dr. Pi, who often attended these meetings, would say nothing or very little, but Madariaga's plans intrigued him. One night Pi, as usual, stayed out of the conversation between Madariaga and the learned men, and, busying himself by studying the various objects that decorated the ample dining room, found himself particularly drawn to a piece of china.

"Valuable china, undoubtedly," he said to himself.

But why had it interested him so much? He approached it, took it in his hands; it was a beautiful piece. But something told him that it was more than artistic value that drew him to the object. The china was in the form of a centaur. Perhaps it was Chiron, the wise.

"A valuable piece, no doubt, Madariaga?"

Madariaga limited himself to a nod and resumed his conversation with the learned men.

"We're already yielding horses that look less and less like horses: their heads, especially, are growing less and less like the heads of ordinary horses."

"Just what is it you're after?" asked Professor Héctor Maldonado.

"It's still too early to say. Carry on with your pursuits in this vein and we'll speak later on."

It was then that Professor von Krausen took the floor.

"We can only accompany you," he said, "up to a certain point in your research, experiment, or however you want to call it. We will give you a certain amount of time—a month, shall we say—and if at the end of this period you do not confess to us the ultimate objective behind all this, we'll announce then and there we have no choice but to abandon you."

"That would be a shame, a real shame, I would have no choice but to resort to less efficient services and that could throw everything into jeopardy."

Dr. Maldonado, now a bit more conciliatory, moved closer to Madariaga.

"You must understand," he said, "that it's impossible for us to work in the dark like this. You must give us some clue to this enigma."

"All right," answered Madariaga, "I'll give you the clue you ask of me: the key to the enigma, as you call it, is in this very room."

The scientists looked around, bewildered. Dr. Pi alone found in those words confirmation of the slight suspicion that had arisen from his study of the china. Now he saw it plainly: the poet Madariaga was planning to bring Chiron the centaur back to life.

Pi said nothing of it. Nor did he make any remark on the matter to the scientists. Other occupations, obligations, or vocations absorbed him. He never found out how the experiments had ended. Pi has an intense, but highly diversified curiosity, that's why we cannot know if today the centaur is merely a piece of china beside a tapestry or if it has been brought back to life, and once again offers advice and counsel. Perhaps Madariaga could say.

The Degroucher

Just outside of Florida, on the narrow Rivadavia, right there, stood the enormous building. Méndez Mosquera was in charge of promotion and publicity, with his style, so much his own and so much his collaborators', which combined subtlety, audacity, fantasy, direct appeal, and ambiguity. And, of course, pure intentions. Clorindo Testa was the architect. The paintings were by Alfredo Hlito.

Ramps, elevators, service lifts, passageways, private offices, computers, kitchens, restaurants, and lots of people: secretaries, women of great and no importance, carports, cars, galleries, people who spoke Javanese and even Spanish. Women, saunas, massage therapists, teleprinters, messengers of all sorts, specialized journalists, lights, darknesses. Lots of glass, lots of transparency: from outside, everything that went on inside was visible, even what happened in the bathrooms and very private bedrooms that certain executives had had specially built. The building was mammoth-sized, it rose, it flew, it got mixed up with the air and induced in people better purposes. Almost like a cathedral.

With respect to the atmosphere, everything had been anticipated: not only the air conditioning—it really was perfect—and the superfunctional music; provisions had gone much further. It happens that Dr. Rentería, in his capacity as human relations specialist, had arranged for the Supreme Council supervising the construction process to approve the acquisition and installation of an extremely strange apparatus: a degroucher.

This apparatus had multiple, complex, and subtle functions. It was supposed to absorb bad moods, aggression, depression, the sarcastic spirit, desperation, pessimism, and even excessive exaltation of any origin within everyone who found themselves inside the building. It was an extremely expensive apparatus and its installation demanded very careful study and the intervention of prestigious specialists in ecology like Tomás Maldonado, who had said, succinctly:

"Do as you like, but first read my book."

The ecological complication arose from the fact that that shower of curses and insults, bad moods, disillusionment, falsehood, unwillingness and indignation had to be expelled, and in a place already oversaturated by similarly negative conditions. The engineer von Ebbing found the solution by installing an auxiliary apparatus designed to transform that shower of curses and like elements into music by Mozart, Kagel, Kröpfl, and Rolando Mañanes.

Everything worked splendidly, inside the building and out. For a time. It happened that one day, Calle Florida, the whole city, was invaded by an avalanche of bad mood, protest, uproar, curses, and insults. The authorities intervened and the apparatus was unplugged, but the bad mood then invaded the entire building and produced a corresponding chaos in its bars, computers, and secretaries.

"It's a disaster," said Mr. Mangini, the building manager.

"You've got to do something. You're the manager, aren't you?" said the president of the board, with a stony smile.

"Yes, yes," answered Mangini, and at that very moment he recalled Dr. Pi. Though it might prove difficult, he would try to find him. He went to a nearby casino. There was Pi, in the company of a brunette. Mangini quickly explained the situation.

"Leave all this and come with me."

"I will not abandon this brunette for anything."

"Fine, bring the brunette, but come straight away."

They rushed right out. By now the building had become the scene of a number of rows and devastations. A brouhaha, in short.

"Where is Dr. Rentería?" asked Dr. Pi.

"What does Dr. Rentería have to do with it?"

"Tell me where Dr. Rentería is or I'm off the case."

They proceeded to Rentería's office, where they found him with an expression of deep satisfaction, in great contrast to the general irritation.

"Who authorized you to come in here without being announced?" asked Rentería.

Pi looked at him fixedly and, holding the blade of his walking stick against his chest, ordered:

"Take us to where you caused the glitch."

"What folly!" said Rentería timidly.

"Come on, let's not waste time. Get up."

Pi held the walking stick at Rentería's back.

"We've got to take the stairs to the fifteenth floor," explained Rentería.

"We'll get there."

"It's just here, behind this door."

They opened it. One of the conveyer belts of the

degroucher was obstructed by a thick iron crossbeam.

"We must proceed quickly. Let's the four of us push the beam off."

That's just what they did and the apparatus resumed normal function.

"My mission is complete; I'm off with my brunette," said Pi.

In and outside the building, good mood, good manners, and even intelligence were restored.

"Excuse me, Pi, but why would Rentería have done this?"

"For the love of glory, or, better yet, for the love of prestige. He wanted to be the one to discover the cause of the problem. I know him well. He's done things like this in the past."

The Return

Dr. Pi returns to Madariaga's cabin. He left something important there. He sees no one's around and the door's half open. He goes in. Stretched out on the floor of the cabin is Dr. Mignini, rich landowner of the region. His throat's been quite recently cut. Atop a bookcase he finds the document he'd been looking for and puts it in his pocket. He hears the sound of steps approaching and retreats quickly, but is seen. He is followed.

He runs to the beach and manages to board the small boat awaiting him.

"Murderer!" they yell.

In the distance the voices are lost. But Dr. Pi thinks he can prove his innocence.

Only later, much later, would he discover that there is no innocence where there is not love.

Universal Levitation

One day, like any other, the performance was about to begin. It was in a small theater in the fairgrounds. A few rows of seats, a stage, a shabby curtain. At the entrance, Dr. Pi attempted to attract passersby via megaphone. Several artists participating in the performance exhibited their skills: the strong man, the fire eater, the amnesiac, and Max, whose supernatural powers could achieve universal levitation. But no one approached the ticket booth. No one was coming. Then Dr. Pi asked Max to do his number, free of charge, and where everyone could see. Upon the announcement, a crowd began to gather.

"I shall offer myself such that Max may exercise his powers upon me."

The doctor lay down on the floor. Max sat at his side and concentrated for a few seconds. Slowly, the Doctor, rigid and closed-eyed, began to rise. He reached the height of the theater's show bill. There he stopped for a moment, only to immediately resume his speedy ascent, after which he disappeared into the clouds. The strongman then grabbed hold of the megaphone and took up expounding the grandness of the performance.

The crowd broke up. No one approached the ticket booth. No one came.

An Old Lady Travels by Bus

The bus leaves the city behind. I have the tickets in my pockets. An old lady sets a brown package on the luggage rack.

"Thank you, thank you."

The bus stops and a man in uniform gets on.

"Here are the tickets," I tell him.

"I'm just looking for a brown package," he replies.

The bus continues through forests and plains. Night falls.

The woman opens the window and takes the package as if to throw it out, but the man in uniform jumps up and grabs it from her. No one has noticed anything. The woman is quiet and closes the window. The trees grow dark. The man in uniform opens the brown package and out comes Dr. Pi in a slightly wrinkled suit.

Staff Recruitment

"Do you need an expeditionary here?" Enrique Lantz asked the pretty secretary.

"We need one. You're the first. Have a seat please. The manager isn't here yet."

Lantz, a young, robust man in a black jacket and thick green glasses, went to sit near the secretary, but she pointed him to a chair by the window.

"You can better admire the view from there. Don't forget we're on the fortieth floor."

"Thank you, thank you, I'll admire the city, I'll admire you. Splendid morning, isn't it?"

"I'm Linda," said the secretary, with a smile. "Isn't that more like what you wanted to ask me?"

"In effect, that and much more. Will you be participating in the expedition?"

"Possibly. It all depends on the itinerary and on the manager," said the secretary, crossing her beautiful legs. "It's nice here, isn't it?"

"Very nice, most definitely."

Lantz got up and walked toward the secretary's desk.

"Not now," said Linda. "First you'll have to fill out a sheet with your personal information. Let's see: may I have your name?"

"Enrique Lantz."

"How did you get up here? The elevator's broken, the stairway's been closed by the Municipal Department of Morality."

"Scaling walls is one of my specialties. I use special shoes and an adhesive walking stick."

"Which expeditions have you participated in? Name the most important."

"To Aconcagua, Orinoco, Matto Grosso, and Palo Santo."

"Which of these words do you most prefer: sedition, folly, archdeacon, or headdress?"

"Headdress."

"Do you believe in the virginity of King Solomon?"

"It appears evident in virtue of the second law of thermodynamics."

"Complete this sentence: The pony was galloping…"

"… after an impossible love."

"A sentence similar to the following: 'The jetplane shortens distances.'"

"The bell-ringer stays in bed."

"What does the word forest mean to you?"

In vain by the forest in the dale
I seek her behind every tree
for she took a mysterious trail
I've never been able to see."[1]

Linda opened one of the drawers of her desk and took out a plate of rice pudding and a small flask of saffron.

"Let's do the rice pudding test. I'm going to sprinkle a little cinnamon on top. You have to tell me what the shape of the cinnamon resembles."

"A canoe adrift."

"Which do you prefer: a scrub or a rub?"

---

[1] From *La flecha de oro* by Miguel Antonio Caro (Colombian poet, philosopher, and politician; 1843–1909). *Trans.*

"A scrub in the morning and a rub at night."

"Speaking of which: let's lie down on the sofa. It is the final test."

Linda and Lantz quickly undressed. Lantz kept his green glasses on and managed to pass the test.

In the meantime, Professor Pi had been climbing up the down staircase to no effect. His mountaineering outfit and the instructions he secretly carried in the pockets of his shiny pants had been of no use: the Professor had not gotten past the third step up from the ground floor and he was meant to go to the fortieth.

Pi pounded on the wall. A shriek was heard, a large gap opened and Pi was sucked into the center of the hole. A few moments later he found himself in the office. Linda ran to embrace him. Together they continued recruiting staff for the expedition.

Don Ascanio and His Trumpet or Madariaga's Cabin

Dr. Pi, with his top hat, tailcoat, and spectacles, has sought refuge in a cabin in the middle of a forest by the seashore. Dr. Pi waits, looking out the only window, indifferent to the days, the wind, and the rumors of summer.

A landing barge slowly approaches. Dr. Pi goes to receive it. He walks into the sea and climbs onto the craft. The scene has been witnessed by Don Ascanio from a nearby cabin.

"It's the perfect moment," says Don Ascanio. "I must warn the poet Madariaga."

And he sounds his trumpet at length, inundating the forest, waking it up, calling, in short, to Madariaga, his friends, the tree, the spring, the squirrel, and the footpath. A new trumpet blare marks the start of the year. The center of the forest lights up. Its inhabitants march toward it to witness the great moment.

Finally, the density of the woodland opens and the poet emerges, freed, smiling, escorted by porcupines, nightingales, anacondas, fauns, alligators, lightfish, myrtles, pines, tuna, mburucuyas, deer, gnats, glow-worms, girls, bulrushes, salts, barrels, canoes, tavern and brothel flyers, castaways, pilgrims, swindlers and saints, falcons, golden orioles, hares, pheasants, shamans, sleeping beauty and the witch, muskets, cloth caps and knapsacks, sailors, fishermen, silver-plated batrachians and nymphs, mats for long siestas and orchids, hydrangeas and artichokes, and great fatigue and lament and birth and death, and the jubilant color and the farewell, and many arms and glasses.

The entourage, led as always by Don Ascanio and his trumpet, marches toward the cabin that Dr. Pi has just left.

"This is the poet's cabin," says Don Ascansio.

Madariaga enters his home and the trumpet sounds for the last time.

The Neighbor

"To hell with your projects and plans! Who would think of living in this godforsaken place! You'll never learn. I'm moving out this instant. The fault is mine for going with a guy like you in the first place."

Elvira left and Carlos continued to stoke the furnace. He had his plans, it's true, and he couldn't abandon them. He would leave, too, but at the right time. Meanwhile, one of the neighbors was watching him, leaning on her balcony. At that moment, Dr. Pi arrived.

"Leave that fire alone now; there are more important things to do. Put on your hat, we're leaving. Don't forget to bring the Burgundians' Chalice. We'll invite your neighbor. She'll come in handy."

The three got mixed up among the masked people on the street. Dr. Pi, who appeared even taller with his top hat, led the way through the crowd. Carlos, clutching onto his neighbor, tried to not lose sight of him.

"Doctor, Edgar is waiting for us in the tower!" Carlos shouted.

"You're mistaken, my friend, he's already at the airport."

They went to a café for a while to rest.

"Just as I suspected," said Dr. Pi. "We've been discovered. But we've still got time to throw them off track: hide the Chalice under your cloak and run away with your neighbor."

The Wait

Dr. Pi boarded the helicopter. Dr. Fortich accompanied him.

"We'll go to a safer place," said Fortich. "We'll fly over the region," he added. "And what's more: we'll land and go to our hideout. There we sort and read correspondence."

But when he saw a red car on the highway, he changed his mind.

"No, landing won't be possible for the time being. Take a few nose dives over that red car," ordered Fortich.

They nearly touched the top of the car two or three times. It came to an abrupt halt and made for the hideout.

"We've got to land, and quick," ordered Fortich.

Too late. The red car had disappeared.

"These people know too much," said Fortich.

They landed.

"We've got to stop these people from contacting the others."

"But how?" asked the pilot.

"We'll blow up the hideout with everyone inside," said Fortich, stroking his bald head. "We must proceed," he added. "I'll go with the pilot. You'll stay here with the stewardess. The apparatus is locked. It'll be impossible to get it going."

Dr. Fortich and the pilot directed themselves resolutely toward the hideout.

"We'll wait for the right moment," said Pi.

"To do what?" asked the stewardess. Then she said, "I'm Linda."

Pi looked at her and liked her immediately.

They turned the radio on, had a few whiskies and talked. Night came slowly. The ground was full of thistle, Jerusalem thorn, and hawthorn. They ate some sandwiches. Several times Pi tried to get the helicopter going to no avail. The music stopped and they heard the voice of Fortich:

"I still have some time. Don't try to escape. Go to bed, make love without soiling the bedspread, and wait."

The Brunette and the Miracle of the Vial

Dr. Pi was alone in the silence of his uncomfortable and narrow room. They were coming to kill him, he knew it. His weapons would not help him this time.

Dr. Pi would not change his plans: he was awaiting a brunette, as was his habit.

They were going to try to kill him. He didn't know why. It would be a sweet, light, discreet, tiptoeing death. But Dr. Pi wasn't worried about that. He had a lot to do, and besides, he was awaiting a brunette.

Dr. Pi lay on his back on his cot and looked at the low ceiling. From there, he thought, the destroying beam will come. But what if the beam carries the brunette in its bag? In that case he could do nothing. He took a giant aluminum umbrella out of the closet and waited confidently for the brunette.

After a while she came in, took a vial out of her bag and threw it onto the umbrella, instantly dissolving it.

"Let's run away," she said, "you made it by a hair."

The Notebook with the Black Cover

At five in the morning Dr. Pi had boarded the train that was now taking him through the prairie. The sun was high when he decided to consult his notebook with the black cover. All was in order, he told himself, closing the notebook. A man on crutches and with no legs entered the carriage selling lotto tickets. The train rounded a curve and the man fell on Dr. Pi. The ticket seller shrieked:

"My tickets, my tickets! They've flown out the window."

"Here they are," said Dr. Pi composedly. "Please give me back my notebook with the black cover."

"Take it. That notebook doesn't have what I'm looking for."

They arrived at Mercedes, in San Luis, and Dr. Pi took a quick stroll through the station. In the waiting room a blonde woman watched him attentively. She was with a bearded, very thin man with black spectacles. He gesticulated, spoke without making any audible sounds, as he had lost his voice, and stomped on the wood floor with the heels of his shoes. He was short and kept getting up from the bench on which he sat. He tried to scream, but no sound came out. The woman looked around distractedly and consulted her watch.

A young girl selling oranges and parsley walked in. The bearded man made a gesture of indignation and threw her out. He continued his stomping. The blonde was barely watching him. She left and boarded the train. The bearded man seemed to grow furious. The parsley and oranges girl once again offered her merchandise. The bearded man kissed her and gave her a fistful of coins. The blonde closed the window. Dr. Pi sat at her side. The blonde embraced him and said:

"Here is your notebook with the black cover."

The Wedding

Dr. Pi had been invited to a wedding on Twenty-third Street. He'd wanted to get there before the newlyweds left so he could give them a gift. The streets were wet, dark, and he was unfamiliar with this part of the city. Dogs barked, loose horses wandered slowly, splashing mud and bits of garbage. A cornet sounded and then a knock on a faraway door. A few more blocks and he'd be at the hotel where the wedding was. Suddenly someone dashed out of the garden of a house.

"Please, help me."

Dr. Pi took out and lit his lantern. It was Lucía, a girl in a multicolored dress and cloaked in a gray, threadbare shawl.

"Of course I'll help you. What do you need?"

"I want to go with you."

"Don't you like it here?"

"No."

Dr. Pi handed her the package he carried under his arm.

"Take this. It'll come in handy. Now come with me."

He offered her his arm and they walked several blocks toward the main boulevard.

"Here we are," said Pi. They stopped before the door of a dilapidated house. Doña Jimena opened the door to let them in.

"I entrust Lucía to you. I'll be back for her later."

Pi headed toward the hotel where the wedding reception was. He greeted the bride and groom. Among the guests he saw the notary Ricciardi. A short, bald, dumpy-looking man with dark glasses, wearing a light-colored, wrinkled and stained suit. He seemed to grow worried upon seeing Dr. Pi.

"I don't want to know anything of your affairs. Here are the bridge plans, you're on your own," he told the notary in a low voice.

Ricciardi asked Doña Jimena to dance a waltz. After taking a few turns, they went out onto the balcony. Lucía, who was waiting in the street, whistled and tossed a package up to the balcony. Dr. Pi hurried to seize it before the notary could get to it. He went out to the street with the package and plans. There he found a very happy Lucía. Together they set out toward the port, indifferent to the drizzle and to the threats of the notary.

The Four Horsemen

Dr. Pi had had a few hassles. His luggage had been stolen and he had even been insulted by a woman who'd mistaken him for her husband. Dr. Pi attempted to console her without correcting her error and accepted all the recriminations, accusations, and misdeeds that she took to be true. Dr. Pi mounted his horse and left without luggage, without wife and with a clear path: He had to find Iadarola at the crossroads.

"Here it is," he said to himself, "I'll wait for him at the inn."

He watched the dark night. His horse, sweaty, rested. He shook the hand of the innkeeper.

"I have no luggage," he said.

"Better that way."

After a little while Iadarola appeared surrounded by two men in ponchos. They embraced.

"We've got to leave right away," said Iadarola.

And the four horsemen took their leave. In the middle of the night, at the break of day. When the sun rose, Dr. Pi suggested they rest under a tree. A willow next to a brook. Lidia appeared with a kettle and *mate*. They kissed.

"Yes, Lidia, that's what I'm getting at," said Dr. Pi, handing her a scapular.

The four horsemen resumed their trek under the sun. They arrived at Trenque Lauquen. There they made the acquaintance of a traveling merchant.

"I think my wife is confused," he told them.

Dr. Pi said nothing.

The four horsemen departed, leaving confusion, baggage, and wind behind. Night was coming.

The Waterfall and the Linguist

Dr. Pi found himself under a waterfall. He had taken refuge there while he waited for Marta. She would be coming any moment. That had been the plan. Pi could hardly see through the water and it was beginning to get dark. "No matter," Dr. Pi told himself. "Marta's arrival will justify everything." And he kept waiting. After a little while, amidst the waters of the waterfall, someone appeared. It was not Marta. It was a linguist, specializing in stylistics, who said, without greeting him:

"First and foremost let us agree that discourse refers to each and every utterance involving a speaker and a receiver."

Dr. Pi took a portable heater and a lantern out of a bag. He sensed the oncoming air and sounds of nightfall.

"Let's take it slow," said Pi.

"And there are various kinds of discourse," continued the linguist. "We have, for example, indirect discourse, and free indirect discourse. Let me clarify," she added, taking a few steps toward him—she was blonde, brimming, with copper-colored skin, tousled hair, and wore a red tunic—"free indirect discourse is produced by the omission of introductory and linking verbs."

"That must be right," said Pi, "but I'm getting wet, it's cold, it's getting dark, I'm waiting for Marta and I'm in the mood to sleep with her."

"Gorgeous styleme," said the linguist, and she moved a little closer to Pi.

Suddenly Marta appeared. The linguist left.

Pi hugged and kissed her and greeted her with these words:

"The defamiliarization of the signifier is not resolved by the degradation of its semantic weight."

The Tandem Bike and the Archarm's Envelope

Dr. Pi, to whom the Archarm had just given the agreed-upon envelope that night on the corner of Corrientes and Montevideo, had to be, as soon as possible, at a certain house in Congreso, where he was expected. It was going to rain. Cabs with passengers drove past. Suddenly a free tandem bike appeared. A young brunette with bare, powerful legs, shorts, and a striped T-shirt, was riding it. Pi signaled to her. The bike stopped.

"Hop on in back and put the envelope and the walking stick in the luggage rack," instructed the driver.

"I'm going to the Congreso neighborhood," said Pi, after heeding the brunette's instructions.

"We'll have to make a detour, there's an official ceremony going on in Plaza del Congreso."

"All right," answered Pi and he began to pedal vigorously.

The girl looked back at Pi and smiled appreciatively. She had big black eyes.

They took Avenida 9 de Julio southward. They were moving more and more lightly. Suddenly the tandem bike began to fly. They passed the Riachuelo. They got all the way to Avellaneda. It began to rain.

"We should be getting back," said Pi.

The girl nodded and turned the bike around. They flew over the Riachuelo again. They passed over bridges, rooftops, highways.

"It's somewhere around here," said Pi. "Let's land."

They landed. It kept raining. They looked at each

other. Pi wanted to pay. The girl did not accept. She sighed, moved toward Pi, and they kissed and embraced for a long time. The bike left.

"Yes, these kinds of voyages generally end this way," thought Pi, walking slowly toward the house where he was expected. He had left the Archarm's envelope and the walking stick in the luggage rack of the tandem-bike-taxi.

The Waltz

Dr. Pi had missed the last train that winter night. It was cold and the station was deserted. He'd have to stay the night in some inn—that is, if there was one in the small town. He'd have no choice but to move through the shadows and out of the small beam of light that shone from the station's only lamppost. He took a powerful lantern out of one of his pockets and began walking through the town's dusty streets. It was a dark, cold, and silent night. Dr. Pi walked slowly, alternately directing the lantern light straight ahead of him and to the sides. He walked on, passing through large pastures; the houses, old, decrepit, seemed abandoned. Dr. Pi blew his whistle for a long time. He stopped in silence. No answer. No sign of life. He then began to sing the waltz "Over the Waves" at the top of his lungs. Suddenly, the windows of a large three-story house lit up; brighter and brighter lights shone from it. Dr. Pi moved closer and clearly heard laughter and music: they were singing and dancing the waltz "Over the Waves." A shot was fired. The bullet had just missed him. The lights went out and the music stopped. Dr. Pi put out his lantern and waited. In a little while the lights went on again in the house. Someone called out to him. It was Adelita.

"I've been waiting for you. Everyone's gone now."

Dr. Pi resolved to spend the night in Adelita's company. He stayed over, in short, in that small town, where he had missed the last train. The last train of that day and of all the days and years to come, as that line was getting torn out and service was to be suspended indefinitely. But other trains, other stations, other adelitas awaited Dr. Pi. Only he would never again, as he had that night, sing and dance the waltz.

Typical Scenes

Dr. Pi gets up from his desk and walks over to the window of his small office. In the house out front, every day, at the same time, he can see a family seated at the table having lunch: the father, the mother, the two children. The father is a man with a big mustache and golden spectacles who eats his soup stiltedly; the woman, slim, with bags under her eyes, watches the servant's every movement.

When lunch is over, the servant clears the table. The man with the big mustache offers his arm to the woman and they exit the dining room by the side door. One of the children, the older one, tall, scraggy, with corn-colored skin and curly hair, seen from the back, seems to be reading a comic book; the younger one, blonde, white, small and chubby, plays with marbles.

Dr. Pi knows the next scene, as it's just the same every day: The dining room suddenly turns into a park. The children disappear. Night falls. Around a large tree, men and women dance naked, holding hands. Dr. Pi then closes the curtain at his window and returns to his desk.

There he finishes writing a letter. He signs it, gets up, and undresses. He opens the curtain, jumps out the window, and aims for the park, where he joins the dancers, jumping and playing a fife.

Dr. Pi, Elena, and the Glitch

Dr. Pi had attended a show at an art gallery, upon the invitation of its beautiful director. It was the opening of an exhibit of work by the painter Standhausen. Although Dr. Pi, as is well-known, enjoyed art and the friendship of artists, and, even more, that of the beautiful gallery directors, his presence at the gallery had little to do with such matters. He was there to fulfill a mission: to monitor the activities of Dr. Alfonso Venancio Del Pradío y Nágera, doctor, engineer, juggler, man of many talents in the most diverse fields, and, by the looks of it, of great emotional stability.

However, something was not quite right in that balanced and powerful spirit. Secretly, very secretly, he hated artists and poets. What had begun as a slight perturbance at individuals who attempted, in his eyes, to make imbalance into a virtue, eventually became a growing and obsessive phobia. Not even the presence, but just the very name of an artist or a poet was enough to tense up his whole face, and set him off on a course of muttered curses and insults. He could only calm down again when his colleagues—Dr. Del Pradío dealt exclusively with colleagues and patients—chanted his name and joined in his affront. But as his phobia grew, his colleagues' acts of solidarity soon stopped working and they were forced to give him sedatives, mustard plaster, poultice, cold compresses, heating pads, and long baths. When Dr. Del Pradío returned to his normal state, he understood that such outbursts were beginning to damage his reputation, not only among his colleagues, but among his patients and even his neighbors.

It was in one of these lucid moments that Dr. Del Pradío resolved to consult his prestigious colleague, Professor Mondragón, an astute, obstinate man with a rapacious and masterful head, who wore dark glasses so as not to have to look anyone in the face, and certainly not in the eyes. He had a nasal voice and a slight stutter.

"Dr. Del Pradío," said Professor Mondragón, after having attentively listened to his colleague's account of disturbances and outbursts, "you are not suffering from a phobia: we all think and feel the same way with respect to the matter you discuss"—for obvious reasons, Professor Mondragón did not want to call the matter by its name— "but it so happens that we have actively introjected this matter, that's why we don't get out of hand like you."

"Actively introjected? Excuse me, Professor, but I don't understand."

"I'll explain it to you," said Mondragón with a condescending smile. "By 'active introjection' of an attitude that is proper, but which can cause us social difficulties, we understand: 1) the relegation of this attitude to the plane of unconsciousness; 2) the projection of this attitude, not in words, but in acts. Or, in other words: not speaking, not getting upset, but rather acting. I'll make it even clearer: it involves destroying—or helping to, for there are already so many doing so—art and poetry and their creators" (here the professor was happy to name both factors because he was now feeling rather sure of himself: his words were having a deep effect on his interlocutor).

"I see," said Dr. Del Pradío. "Thank you, Professor," he added. "Yes, now I see it all very clearly. Yes, yes, act, not speak, not get upset, act, completely exterminate the abhorrent imbalance, the forms that materialize out of the last remnants of man's morbid unconscious. Now I understand, thank you, thank you." Dr. Alfonso Venancio Del Pradío y Nágera then broke out in a peal of laughter that grew steadily louder, insistent, and almost uninterrupted.

That is how Professor Mondragón left him, tiptoeing and saying lowly: "Catharsis." Dr. Del Pradío was cured and would take action.

And so it was on account of the results obtained and that very action that Dr. Pi found himself in the gallery. There had already been several outrages in galleries, museums, libraries, bookstores, concert halls, music shops. As a matter of fact, the destroyed or deteriorated objects were not always of great value, but the mission entrusted to Dr. Pi on this occasion was not so much to authenticate the works affected by the destructive act, as much as to quash, wherever possible, that very act, whether it was exercised upon the artwork or upon the spirit of the people.

Dr. Pi was sitting in front of Elena, looking into her eyes, his hands wrapped around and resting on his walking stick. She looked back at him steadily. He was trying to see some of the much that was in her eyes. He was—they were—almost in a trance. But something forced Dr. Pi to leave this almost trance. He had seen, through a stained-glass window, the figure of a very heavy, half-hunched and broad-scalped man, wearing a dark and wrinkled suit, and carrying a large yellow package under his arm.

Pi leapt up. Elena followed.

"It's Dr. Alfonso Venancio Del Pradío y Nágera, renowned specialist..." began Elena.

"We're acquainted," said Pi.

"Dr. Pi! What a pleasure to see you!" said Del Pradío with a hint of anguish as he tried to conceal his immense package.

"I didn't know you were an art lover, Dr. Del Pradío," observed Pi.

"Well, I am, but you two continue your conversation; I'll go explore the exhibit."

"And I'll accompany you, Dr. Del Pradío. It'll be my pleasure," said Pi.

Elena left them for a few moments as they explored the exhibit.

"Innocence is the world's worst ill," Dr. Del Pradío suddenly declared. "It's the sickness par excellence."

Dr. Pi said nothing, though he seemed to nod lightly. Dr. Del Pradío then began to abound in arguments in favor of his thesis. He was so enthused that, in a moment of carelessness, he dropped the package. Pi quickly picked it up and tossed it out an open window. An explosion was heard.

"Why did you do that, Pi? Why?" screamed Del Pradío as he fled down the stairs.

"What happened?" asked Elena, alarmed.

"That man wanted to destroy the gallery and everyone in it."

"Is it possible? He seemed like such a wise man…"

"The worst part is that he's bound to return, but do not be alarmed; I've got it all worked out."

"In that case it would be better to not let him in."

"We'll let him in. I know his methods. Soon he'll try to produce a trivial glitch in the electrical device and then he'll leave, satisfied. He will have achieved the task he's assigned himself today. I've come supplied with everything necessary for the repairs."

A little while later Dr. Del Pradío reappeared.

"I'm sorry for the confusion before," he stammered.

"It's nothing, Doctor, continue enjoying the artwork," replied Pi.

A few moments later, the gallery went dark. The sound of laughter and the hurried steps of a man's stumbling escape was heard.

"Ladies and gentlemen," said Elena, addressing the spectators, "I ask that you excuse this disruption. It's a technical glitch that will be remedied in just a few minutes. Soon you'll be able to resume enjoying the show. Meanwhile drink up the contents of your glasses."

Pi took Elena's hand and, with the help of his powerful lantern, headed toward a small room at the back of the house, where the switchboards were. When they got there, Pi put his lantern, his tool kit, and his walking stick down and took Elena into his arms. There was a very long, interminable kiss. Screams of protest were heard from the spectators. The interruption was going on too long.

Pi stepped out of Elena's embrace and said:

"Let's repair that glitch."

The Mix-Up

Dr. Pi was going be late to his date. He had had various difficulties descending the mountain. Avalanches, insistent salespeople, a snake, and a broken leg. But in the end, Pi arrived at the agreed-upon shack. He put his leg in a splint, walked toward the fire and awaited his friends, who arrived not too long after. Dr. Pi greeted them warmly and asked immediately for the rubber boat.

"Here it is," said Dr. Rentería.

"It's got to be inflated. I'll go with Felisa and you keep watch from here."

"It's dangerous for you to go in these conditions," said José, the cook on the expedition.

"Don't worry, nothing can happen to me so long as I'm with Felisa. Lantz is waiting for me in the valley. We've got to take back the Burgundians' Chalice."

Dr. Pi, limping, left the shack with Felisa. Nearby was the fast-flowing river. And the sun. And the dissolving snow. And the green on the other side of the river, and the white and so much blue and so much shadow in the hollow.

Dr. Rentería stopped inflating the boat.

"It is enough," said Pi.

Felisa and Pi got on the boat. Dr. Rentería unmoored it and the two of them, Felisa and Pi, were on their way toward the valley. There they thought they would find Lantz.

They would not find him: Lantz had been kidnapped by Centoira, the cunning skin and hide dealer.

Sir Harrison and Solitude

Sir Harrison Rex Burley de Gongaza, it was said, had been murdered. A man of immense fortune, owner of extensive rail networks in developing nations, proprietor of ships that navigated known and unknown waters, proprietor also of airlines, finance companies, a meteorologist, he was burly, tall, of imposing nose and bulging green eyes; he had a slight stutter and used to click his tongue whenever something worked out for him or didn't.

He had become a friend of Dr. Pi's on account of the construction of a tunnel beneath the Dardanelles Straits. Harrison had named him construction supervisor. Pi had accepted with the condition that his responsibilities be short in duration, as he was not given to taking up permanent positions. Dr. Pi turned out to be efficient, he assisted in construction management and procedures, and buried, at the bottom of the straits, a trunk with a photo of Sir Harrison inside.

On his excursions to London, Pi stayed at Harrison's Tudor palace. There he was given a sumptuous room with balconies overlooking the park that Harrison called Ernest.

Harrison thought himself well-versed in painting. He had a gallery and museum, where one could appreciate a Turner right next to a Vitellone, an Arcimboldo beside a Caravaggio, a Bouguereau next to a Münch, a Calchaquí pictograph next to a thermos of *mate*. Young and pretty women and agile old ladies and even experts were there to explain it all: from an obsolescent smoking jacket that Sir Harrison himself had donated to the museum, to a very weathered bedroom slipper, whose museum tag indicated it had been the property of Anatole France.

One very fluffy and very old bed, with a canopy, had no museum tag. That's where Professor Pi liked to rest, but, on Sir Harrison's advice, before lying down, he always pushed a red button located under the bed. It happens that, on one occasion, Pi forgot to push the button: After a little while, an opulent lady with long blackish hair got into bed naked beside him. Her name was Juana. The bed slowly began to rise and sharp knives emerged from the ceiling. Dr. Pi satisfied his bedmate. It was then that the bed and the knives came to a halt.

"It'll be better," said Pi, after Juana had stopped telling the story of her life, "if we get out of this bed. It's a bit odd," he added, pointing to the knives. "What we've done here, we could do just as well on the floor."

Juana agreed and they continued making love on a rug.

Harrison watched everything from a secret hiding place. When he thought it fit, he approached the lovers and congratulated them.

"Those knives are awful," explained Harrison, "but they stop when the couple in the bed ejaculate, as you did, at just the right time. Not too early, not too late. I'll demonstrate for you. Or maybe that's not necessary: you yourselves have done the demonstration. This piece of furniture," he added with a hint of erudition and patriotism, "was in the Tower of London for a long time, and there lent important services to the British crown. Well, let's leave these innocent artifices and distractions, and Dr. Pi, you resume your work in the Dardanelles Straits."

Pi left in the direction of the Dardanelles, and it was upon his return that he learned of the death of Sir Harrison Burley de Gongoza, which had occurred just moments before the Professor's arrival.

It seems that Harrison had gotten into the canopy bed without taking the proper precautions. The bed had risen and the sharp knives had lowered, coursing through him in various parts of his body. No woman, natural or supernatural, had appeared at his side. Or if one had appeared —according to some experts and connoisseurs of Sir Harrison's customs and highly selective criteria—she must have been rejected.

Harrison was alone and naked: Undoubtedly this was not a game for loners.

The Balcony and the Garden

This balcony looks out onto a garden. My desk sits in front of the balcony, such that I can gaze on the flowerbeds in the garden. I can see the roses, the fountain, and, at dusk, a woman dressed in green who hides behind the trees toward the back. The garden has paths and there is an abandoned wheelbarrow in the corner. In the morning I open the window to the balcony and let my papers fly. This very paper I've just written on. Because what matters, what truly matters, is neither the papers nor my justifications. What matters is the balcony, the garden, and at times the woman.

The Arrival

"We'll be arriving sooner than we thought," said a corpulent man with gray sideburns.

An inconvenience? An advantage?

"I'll have to wait two days at the port," said the man. "It's annoying."

Another traveler in a silver scarf, with a walking stick and glasses:

"For me it's an advantage: I'll set off sooner, I'm just afraid of making a mistake."

"That's why I won't think of leaving the port until two days go by."

All Love is a Now

"We've seen each other before, haven't we?" she said, taking a seat by his side on a bench on the deck of a boat that had just left port.

"Before? Of course, of course," he replied, "but what's unsubstitutable is this now."

The Perfect Angler

The angler has come to sit on the riverbank. He has left his rod aside, with a metal box and a basket. He sits still looking into the distance, while the waters flow into the neighboring pond. The angler is almost absent, he awaits nothing. A canoe emerges in the distance. A young woman rows gracefully. She approaches. She smiles and goes by. The angler has forgotten the name of the woman moving toward the pond and resumes looking into the distance. A hunter emerges from the hills and fires his arm. The angler falls into the river and the reddened waters carry him to the pond, to the nameless woman awaiting him.

Mr. Roux

A retired official takes refuge from the rain in the waiting room of a funeral parlor. I greet him and cross the street, taking advantage of the green light. It is Mr. Roux, I tell myself. The same one who takes advantage of the green light and the waiting room and even funeral parlors. Mr. Roux is also a sculptor. Of course a sculptor is hardly anything. Building a house is something. Giving orders, stacking bricks, exposing yourself to the sun and to wine, buying a new shirt: that's what's important. But the sculpture grows and becomes important when we forget about it. Like the house and the sun. Like a good morning spoken haphazardly to Mr. Roux.

The Political Poet

The poet was a politician as well. He was interested in people's problems, large and small, and was capable of finding and applying solutions. His generosity was efficacious. He could sustain a company. He could master small details. He could enunciate, expound. His eloquence surpassed imposture, and the poet managed to blend in among good and simple people. But if the poet paid attention to matters of the word, beyond the word, feeling he was simply living, he also felt the urgency of the word itself. He also experienced the need to slow down, to break up the fluency between himself and the world. Then the poet began to speak for himself in an attempt to speak better, deeper, and to all men. And he lost his voice and broke his instrument. That's how it was, that's how it always shall be.

Final Act

Mr. R. and his wife have left the theater before the performance is over. The cold is intense. The couple walks slowly. When they get to a corner a young, poorly dressed girl asks them the time. Mr. R. answers with a small smile: it's the time of dreaming.

So the young girl walks to the theater, goes through the stage door and steps through the curtains, where she delivers her lines in the work's final act. Mr. and Mrs. R. continue on their walk.

Miracles of Poverty

My friend Isaiah needed a job. So he published an ad: young ambitious man, enthusiastic, skills, telephone: ... No one could tell if it was a job-offered or job-wanted ad. And replies began to fall from the skies: truly moving cases. Inexplicable deferrals. Talented youths, full of potential, who for one reason or another had been left behind. He couldn't really offer them the work they needed, but at least he could answer their letters, ease some of their worries, give them some hope... And at this Isaiah spent his entire youth, which he could have dedicated to building something for himself.

Transparency

Behind a great glass window, a pretty blonde crippled girl sits sunbathing on a wheelchair. I stop in front of her for a few moments, without really noticing her, to check that I've got some papers in my small case. Yes, I've got them. So I glance up and look at the girl. She smiles at me. I smile at her and walk away briskly. Later, a woman on her way back from the market, with a basket full of vegetables, also stops without noticing her, to arrange her things, until she sees the girl, and they both smile. The woman leaves and the girl resumes sitting alone, smiling. This has been enough for me to see, in a fleeting, full moment, that this world and the other are a single thing, a single mystery, a single moment.

Dulioto

He had left his house early. He got off the tram at Avenida Beira Mar and Machado de Assis and walked to Calle Catete.

He arrived at the house. There was his boss, the Doctor. There were close to fifteen people in the main hall. Dulioto went into one of the inner rooms with some newspapers and books. The Doctor called him.

"Dulioto, do you have those documents?"

"Here they are."

The Doctor was short and fat. He was sweating.

"We've got to open that window," he said.

"It must stay shut, understood? It's for Guimaraes' wife," he was told.

Apologize for the distraction. It was true. Guimaraes' wife's cold constituted a well-known phenomenon.

Aracy brought him a cold glass of guarana.

"Thank you, dear," and he smiled at her slightly.

Important solutions from one moment to the next.

"Dulioto, what did Vieira tell you?"

"Still no news."

Open the window. A well-dressed man was thinking the same. But, of course, it was impossible. There was no need to expose Mr. Guimaraes' wife.

"It's a shame we can't agree on the principal point."

Then the Doctor began an exposition in slightly incorrect Portuguese. He paused and said:

"Dulioto, you can proceed to the garden, if you wish, but be mindful of the wiring."

"I'd like to walk about Flamengo with Aracy."

The falcons were tied up in the back of the house. A young dark man whistled a samba and drummed on a box of matches. His name was Bento.

"Do you know this one?"

He was from Bahia. He began to sing and dance.

"Want to come to a party tonight in Cascadura?"

Dusk came and the garden was almost completely dark. Aracy's room lit up. The window was open, and the girl, lying on her back on the bed, half-naked, was reading a book, holding it up with both hands. Dulioto approached and invited her for a walk about the garden.

> HOW SIMPLE, SIMPLE EVERYTHING SEEMED! I THREW A CHANGE OF CLOTHES, A COUPLE OF BOOKS, SOME PAPERS, NOTHING MORE, IN A SMALL SUITCASE AND I LEFT. AFTER WALK-ING A FEW BLOCKS I FOUND MYSELF IN LARGO DA LAPA. HOW SIMPLE, SIMPLE EVERYTHING SEEMED!

From one of the windows on the top floors emerged Vieira's enormous head.

"Where have you been, my good man? Have you brought the documents?"

"Yes, I've got them with me."

"Before anything, allow me to congratulate you. And now go to the parlor where the Doctor needs you urgently."

When he got to the parlor he found the Doctor playing cards with a group of men in shirtsleeves. They had opened the window.

"Please be so kind as to take a seat. Gordilho the notary wishes to ask you a few questions."

The notary was a man of dark skin and light eyes. Smiling, he pulled his chair toward Dulioto's.

"We do not wish to reproach you for your adventures on Calle General Camara."

The notary interrupted himself and spoke in a low voice to the Doctor. Aracy came in and handed Dulioto a coconut milkshake.

"We were expecting you today in Cascadura," he whispered.

The Doctor stood up:

"Our conversation has been interrupted. Guimaraes' wife has doubts and has retreated. The presence of this distinguished lady was indispensable for the positive outcome of our negotiations. She presided over our meetings with the sensible purpose of preventing any misunderstanding to impede the merger of our two companies. Her absence constitutes a major obstacle for the initial negotiations. Her son, the Excellent Mr. Luiz Affonso Guimaraes Salles de Albuquerque, seems to be reluctant about the merger. If he were to head the company, we would be obliged to leave our projects aside. But there is a solution: find Mr. Affonso Senior, whom you advised, at a bad time, to leave his wife and his managerial duties to the company in order to conduct research of various types among Ecuadorian Indians. A grave error that you, Sir, may correct. Father, would you like to help us to find Don Affonso Guimaraes?"

Minutes of silence. Dulioto said yes. He would do what he could. Gordilho the notary gave him a hug. Milton invited Dulioto to follow him. They went into a spacious bathroom where they found some flight attendants.

"Come through here, please," said Milton, opening a small door.

Once Dulioto had gone through, they shut and locked the door. He found himself completely in the dark. He carefully stretched a leg and found nothing to rest it on. He tossed a penknife: a distant noise. He managed to kneel at the threshold. He grabbed onto the door handle and peered through the keyhole.

Milton and the flight attendants were talking animatedly. He pounded on the door. Hurried steps and someone turned the key. He lowered the latch and leapt into the bathroom, which was also completely dark.

Moments of silence. The flight attendants and Milton were there. Someone lit a lantern, which Dulioto kicked. "This has got to end once and for all." A shot did not hit the target. Dulioto hit Milton with a candelabra. The flight attendants leapt onto Dulioto and tossed him into the emptiness. He let himself fall, drawing up his legs until he ricocheted into the mesh of a net.

I USED TO VISIT AN ALAGOAN GIRL.
SHE LIVED IN IPANEMA AND TWICE A
WEEK I USED TO MAKE THE INTER-
MINABLE JOURNEY ON THE TRAM.
THE GIRL WORKED IN A CAFÉ ON
AVENIDA RIO BLANCO. I DIDN'T

KNOW WHAT WAS GOING ON. SHE
LIVED ON THE RUA DO RIACHUELO.
HER WINDOW LOOKED OUT ONTO
THE MORRO SANTA TERESITA. THERE
WAS A CIRCUS ON THE CORNER.

A door opened. Two men helped him out of the net. There were a fair number of people on the patio, mostly girls. Some of them were Aracy.

"Take him to my room," she said.

They passed through several bedrooms, a large kitchen, and a bathroom.

"It's here."

A little while later Ms. Dorita came, a blonde and opulent lady, and the doctor. Dr. Zisturdo opened a small suitcase and took out some pants.

"We're in Copacabana," he said.

A sharp sound shot out from the corner. A whistle. There was a group of people moving in different directions. The sky was an intense red, broken up here and there by clear patches. The most varied objects were brought from the beach in a large storehouse, whose entryway was the mouth of a giant head. The long bristles in the holes of its nose reached the sky. The sea was angry; at times giant waves washed over a cage on whose roof some monkeys were dancing.

Numerous animals moved about freely without anyone noticing. Many had extraordinary shapes and came out of a ditch full of water that surrounded a construction. Some that looked like fish, but with feet, jumped from great heights. There were also vipers of considerable length, with wings and feet on both ends. Some human heads, completely bald, with an arm on one side and a leg on the other, moved about quickly. The arm, which was much longer than the leg, ended in a talon. The heads threw stones of all sizes at the ditch, over which there slowly lowered a drawbridge, traversed by some people in white overalls transporting laboratory instruments.

When one section of the sky began to clear up, until taking on the shape of a circle, Gordilho the notary descended on a rope.

"What are you doing here?" he asked Dulioto.

"I'm looking for Mr. Guimaraes."

"This doesn't seem like the right place. The fact is that you are compromising the interests of Ms. Dorita by staying in the room of one of her pupils."

"I invited him," said Aracy.

"In the end, I'm not the one to judge all this. House regulations stipulate that in cases such as these, for the purposes of judgment, a tribunal must convene, comprised of the three oldest clients, and presided over by Ms. Dorita."

The notary climbed up the rope and disappeared. Aracy and Dulioto headed toward the deliberation room. On the bench sat the tribunal made up of Gordilho the notary, Vieira, and Milton, presided over by Ms. Dorita. The doctor was the prosecutor.

THE BRUNETTE I LIKE WEARS A ROSE IN HER HAIR. MORA APT. NUMBER ON RUA DO RIACHUELO. I NEEDED TO

TALK ON THE TELEPHONE BUT A
GIRL WORKING AT EL CARIOCA WAS
USING IT. WE MADE FRIENDS. WE
STROLLED ALL NIGHT. I FELT VERY
FREE AND I THREW MYSELF ON THE
SAND.

The doctor began to interrogate Aracy:

"My dear, tell the truth. It's the only thing that can help you. Is this gentleman the individual who surprised you in your bedchamber?"

"He didn't surprise me. I invited him in," answered Aracy.

"Very well, that is all," said the doctor.

The tribunal deliberated a few moments. Finally Ms. Dorita stood up and read the verdict:

"The regulations have been given not only to protect the interests of the House and its clientele, but also to safeguard the security and well-being of its boarders. With regard to such prescriptions of the regulations and to the major transgression represented by the unauthorized presence of Mr. Dulioto in Aracy's bedchamber, the Tribunal has resolved to apply the maximum penalty possible. Milton will be charged with executing it."

Milton accompanied Aracy and Dulioto to an elevator. They went up to the fortieth floor. Bento received them.

"The ceremony is about to begin," he said.

The sea was calm now, but the sky was still red. Reflectors had been installed in the storehouse that now illuminated a plank. Several live hens flew out from one of the storehouse's windows and Shirtz took care of grasping them in the air. Near the ditch they'd installed several school benches. The heads helped to transport the hens from the storehouse to the plank. Someone began to play the cithara and the tambourine. The music and the singing stopped. A man stood up on the plank. It was Mr. Affonso Guimaraes.

Valerio

Valerio had not two, not five, but four legs. Vigorous, fluttering, quick, enrapturing, loving, and skilled. He was, by trade, a tamer. And he tamed with two legs at a time, casting the damp reticulated pizzle, with its sponged pendants fidgeting up and down, onto the sweaty colliding hides, punishing at once the colt's lips and hindquarters.

In general, he never used the four legs all at once: first, two, and then, when they tired, the others.

He could also work on the neck with two feet forward, and let the other two feet work on the flanks. The pony always ended up giving in. He learned to listen and obey Valerio. But not only to Valerio. That was the problem with his taming technique. And for that reason he had increasing trouble finding work. His interminable periods of inactivity were damaging to his occupational talents. Professionally he declined. And so it went until ultimately no one wished to contract his services. Not even for entertainment. Overqualified, Valerio had remained unemployable in life.

Like Belerofonte, at the end of his life, he drew the hatred of the gods, and gave in to melancholy, wandering the desert, avoiding all contact.

Finished Business

He walked slowly down the main street stepping in the dirty snow fifteen blocks long they say and small shops and snow-capped mountains. Southernmost in the world. Inspector Morando had arrived in Ushuaia to work on the Alberini case on his way to handle routine cases: you think it's easy just possible. Fifteen blocks long and five blocks wide before the bay. And he walked comfortably, not even cold, with his jacket, his wind hat, his rubber shoes.

There Alberini would be waiting for him, before the fireplace in his house. His is an old story. It is recorded, buried. They walked slowly. Before leaving Buenos Aires Morando had told Elena: Everything I did I did for you. She had just stood there looking at him. And Morando had gone to the airport. A well-recorded story. And Alberini: I know, sir, but it isn't right. Elena thinks I know nothing. I acted as though I knew nothing. It's better. It's better.

It happened and that's that, why qualify it? It's a useless effort besides it's been so long I could have gotten used to it I haven't gotten used to it worse for you I have the right to know why I've been relocated I want to hear from my family another family's formed here for years it's gone on as though I've accepted the new situation I haven't ever stopped complaining I've explained in writing and verbally my situation an infinite number of times and never to any effect that's how it is some inspectors have listened to me like yourself others have refused to even receive me and yet you insist I don't lose hope I'd like to lose it I can't you write letters no one answers you lodge complaints no one hears and it never occurs to you to think.

And just what is it that I know? What is it she knows? In the world, the sky, the moon and sun have their cups full of the wine of your being. You are free of the world and the world is nothing but you. You are outside of space and space is full of you.

They walked slowly, not feeling the cold. Might have thought once that your situation has no resolution at all definitive why? you yourself say your efforts have been to no effect for years and for years you've repeated the same rationale the same arguments and nothing's happened if I were you I would have convinced myself by now that there's nothing to be done I need someone to tell me why things have happened this way why I was relocated why my letters don't arrive or go unanswered why they won't receive me I'll take a note of complaint you are an engineer yes sir I was chief engineer of the construction of the underwater tunnel how long ago were you relocated? twenty years what position do you currently hold? assistant at the Ushuaia post office.

The first image of old Joaquin: leaning on the bar, glass in hand, standing up straight despite his age (much younger than he seems), tall, slim, with a shabby but ironed suit and a patched-up clean shirt. Merely an ingenious journalist? or more? because sometimes—and not because he's decided it for himself, because he's chosen such a thing, consciously —it would seem that he is (has grown to be) a man who acts in accordance with a secret, lucid, fruitful answer. A man "who knows." Such undoing of so much peripheral disquiet and such giving in to deep experience that he has nearly made it into a profession.

They never gave you any explanation? never and to what do you attribute the relocation? I haven't the slightest idea did you have any problems in your work? on the contrary just days before my relocation I had been congratulated by the public works department it was practically all done I'll draw up the report will I get an answer? do you really need one? after so many years it's likely that deep down I don't expect or need any answer you need to ask that's for sure I need the answer I need everything to be clear and make sense like before.

"You've arrived on time. Help yourself."

"Thanks, old buddy."

There were people there: men and women of all ages, drinks, music. It was hot and most of the guests were cooling off on the large balcony.

A bald man with a piercing voice was doling out insults. He was thin, tall, washed-up, nervous. In almost all of his sentences: shit or stupid. Once in a while he farted.

The group on the balcony talked a little bit about cinema, politics. Then the group waned. The chats grew more intimate. The bald man said shit one more time and left.

There are those who accept you're one of those who questions I don't think so either anyone would question in my case a rebel what are you up to? I'm simply an inspector can you answer me? I'm speaking to you it's my job get me out of here I can't I don't want to but someone does who? the strange thing is that for you I'm the sick one not them their health or illness is another problem it's not your problem so you recommend health to me it's the only thing you can say when you have to say something as in this case it's best clearly to not say anything but you need to say things and have things said back to you.

One morning during Carnival, near Floresta, Carmona and I, after a dance, walked in search of a bus and rounding a corner we ran into a bum. A little old man, wrinkled, wrapped in shredded white sackcloth (some sort of punchinello costume).

"And what happened to the rest of the troupe?"

"They left. Someone made a pot of coffee on a wagon and everyone went their way."

"What do you do in the troupe?"

"I dance."

The man starts to dance, barely moving. He lightly shakes his arms, his legs. He tilts his head. He has no strength. It looks like he's going to fall down. He continues.

"All right, here you go." (Carmona throws him some coins.)

The man carries on as if nothing's happened.

So? nothing and the others? I've already told you it's not their business if all this hounding me helps you somehow it won't help the others look I want to speak to you on another matter forget I'm an inspector it'll be better when I saw him I had the impression for a moment he was going to propose one of those conversations but then the tone of my words disappointed him understand that there are professional duties that there's no choice but to fulfill it's true that those duties give one a sort of support one feels recognized people say there goes the inspector they expect me to do certain things in a certain way and when I do them I experience a sense of fullness, of having a destiny, it is a moment of privilege that is repeated every day however the job is not everything at other times one wants and needs to simply be a man and understand.

The injustice committed upon don Joaquin was obvious. They had undermined the importance of his work: not only was he responsible for establishing and collecting toll fees, he also had to oversee the behavior and volume of the water, its mobility, its growth, its decline. He knew how it spread, how it reached every point in the valley.

That injustice—there was no doubt—would need to be remedied.

Meanwhile don Joaquin stayed by the water. He went in, and before opening a floodgate, he always explained the rationale behind his decision.

He never complained. He remained calm in his post, attuned, surely, to the smallest indications of change.

There was, to be sure, a de facto situation. A punishment. An allegation. A coldness. A hatred. An oblivion. An indifference. Power existed and that was the total explanation possible.

But what did don Joaquin care about the logic of power? Why anticipate his impulses, his decisions and his sudden and failed logic? What does any of this have to do with the freedom of the waters?

And that's how don Joaquin began to gather the fruits

of the air, to depend less and less on the changes. That's
how he began to sing, to go out at night.

I am familiar with this that fullness suddenly everything ended it has begun discoveries proof I'll go the same
I'll get out I'm sure I hope they walked slowly, their situation something definitive.

Epilogue

A Man Scales the Walls and Goes Up to Heaven

Hanging from a rope
the man who scales walls
has strong shoes with nails
He scales the walls
because he's forgotten the keys to his house
and as he scales the walls
to the thirteenth floor
he stops a few moments
on the balcony of each floor
where he takes in the smell of the geraniums
the honeysuckles
the hydrangeas
and the daffodils
It's sunny
ship flags
traveling merchants
and beyond is the river
and beyond the bridges
that lead to the pampa
Below are children
coming out of school
and planes and birds pass in the sky
and hats with wide brims
that the wind blew from the unprepared
The rope has been tied to the beam
that sticks out over the roof
The man ties it to his belt
and ascends taking in the rope with his gloved hands

He wears a floral vest and a checkered hat
He has to get to the thirteenth floor
where he must water some carnations
mash some corn
write some letters
and cook a stew
He goes up slowly
and stops a bit on each floor to rest
He goes onto the balcony on each floor
and sits in a chair
or stretches out on the deck furniture
and talks to the neighbor or neighbors
and accepts a coffee or *mate*
and lets a stream of wine fall from his canteen
into his throat
or plays cards
or listens to secrets and gives advice
and talks about some episode in his life
until he waves goodbye and leaves
and continues scaling the walls
hanging from a rope
It's the man who has strong shoes with nails
and a floral vest and checkered hat
who forgot the keys to his house
and takes in the smell of the geraniums
and has to get to the thirteenth floor
before the owls come out
and the windows light up
The birds and the river are far away
and the grass in the park

and the horses galloping in the fields
and his dilapidated chair
and the out of order
bathtub
full of dirt and flowers
and the sea and the approaching ship
and the lizard hiding in the rocks
and the newspaper man who from below
yells to him warnings and advice
as the man flies
he ascends
he conquers each floor with effort
and always looks up
The ground is far away
The sky is far away
The man who scales the walls
hanging from a rope
when he enters a house by the balcony
is well received by the neighbors
and he tries to make himself useful
But in one of the houses
an unexpected woman
who is only one woman
and at the same time
all the women in his life
asks him to bring her along
so she ties herself to the rope too
and goes up with the man past the thirteenth floor
toward the clouds
the open air

the sky
the wind
among the geraniums
the umbrellas
the deck furniture
over bridges and newsstands
and posts and plants
and some drops
and seeds
and dreams
with his checkered hat
with his floral vest
with his all-time sweetheart

Translator's Afterword

The poet Enrique Molina's introduction to the 1983 *Último Reino* edition of *Vida y memoria del Doctor Pi* proffers a thorough and well-reasoned description of the doctor's background, powers, and inimitable appeal, tracing and praising Pi's uncanny knacks for unflinchingly resolving conflict of elusive dimension with a bewinking ease; for taming the ridiculous personages who have somehow gained credibility in his midst; and for unswervingly negotiating the absurdity sprung up all around him, all while rarely neglecting to catch the attention of a woman with an allure to rival his own.

Molina's just praise of Pi's suavity points to that of his maker; and in many ways, Pi's unruffled handling of quotidian absurdity is actually outdone by Bayley's dexterous handling of language, and its materiality. The feat—this *"administración de la materialidad del lenguaje"*—was the overt object of study, practice, and eventual mastery for Bayley throughout the steady course of his career, which spanned the larger part of the twentieth century and impacted, indelibly, the Argentine literary landscape. Though Bayley published plays, essays, and translations, and (co-)founded some of his epoch's most influential magazines and movements, he was predominantly a poet, and engaged foremost by language's potency and plasticity, which he honored and operated, respectively, under his innovative *invencionista* aesthetic. Pi represents his sole publication in prose, a genre in which he could gracefully contrive the ridiculous unbeffudledly, with an unusual blend of linguistic quirk and eloquence. It is with these qualities that I hope he now travels into English.

—Emily Toder